BELLE

A FRACTURED FAIRY TALE

By

J.E. Taylor

Belle: A Fractured Fairy Tale © January 2023
J.E. Taylor

Can a cursed shifter find the love needed to be cured?

My name is Belle, and I was looking forward to finding my mate at the annual Shifter's Ball. Unfortunately, my petty side had to strike out at a homely patron who was not dressed for a ball. She looked more like the one hired to pick up after the horses. And I said so, loudly, as my friends snickered at my dark wit.

That's when karma struck.

That homely patron wasn't as she seemed. She was a powerful sorceress who laid a vanity curse on me, which made me partially shift into this monstrosity that pulls screams from grown men and cringes from my family and friends.

If I had just kept my cruel words to myself, I would not be exiled to my grandfather's dilapidated estate, searching for a way to break this curse without getting killed in the process.

BELLE Chapter 1

I STIL REMEMBER THE evening I was changed into this hideous thing. It was the night of the Shifter's Ball, where I should have met my potential mate. Instead, I was hanging with a group of my friends, making fun of the guests. One in particular was so out of place, she begged to be mocked.

I was the instigator. Snickering loud enough to be heard by this hideous woman. I commented on her drab choice of gown for such an occasion. It was as if she just grabbed any old thing to sling over her shoulders. Her posture didn't help, neither did her unwashed and unkept hair that looked like a rat's nest with stray string hanging out of it in no real order.

It was as if the girl had not bothered to make herself presentable for something as important as the Shifter's Ball.

Little did I know, she was a witch and not a shifter.

And she had a terribly mean streak when it came to bullies.

She spun on me and pointed her gnarled finger, hissing words in a language I did not understand. Guttural sounds fell from her mouth, and her eyes blazed as if her soul were on fire. Black smoke shot from her finger, and when it hit my chest, my entire form bowed backward with the pain.

But no sound escaped my tight throat. Not a scream and not a howl. My defenses kicked into gear, and I shifted. At least, that's what I thought was happening.

My left hand formed into a wolf's paw, my claws extended and sharp. My snout elongated, and my teeth became razor points in my mouth. My skin tingled where patches of fur sprouted. My left ear pulled, forming into a canine ear, itching as it grew. My right leg shortened to a canine leg, tilting me to the side.

And then everything stopped. My shift froze between human and wolf, and the smoke surrounding me settled into my skin.

My friends gasped and shrank away from me.

The crone continued to point, but now she wore a spiteful smile. "Now you are as ugly as your family's spirit." She waved her hands, and a glass box appeared in my arms, with a beautiful rosebush with dozens of roses ready to bloom enclosed inside. "You have until the last petal falls to find someone to love you. If you fail, you will remain as you are for the rest of eternity."

And with a puff of white smoke, she disappeared.

I looked at my human hand and my partially shifted arm in horror and turned, fleeing to the restroom. In the candlelit stall, I stared at the mirror, wondering when I would wake from this horrifying nightmare.

BELLE Chapter 2

INSTEAD OF GOING BACK into the ball in this state, I ran—if you could call it that. It was more of a lumbering jog that looked more monstrous than I felt. I barged through the front door of my home at the time the ball would have been at full steam, with mates dancing with each other. A part of me wanted to howl my pain, but my mouth would not form the right way to bay my sorrow to the full moon above. My parents turned from their reading chairs and gasped, jumping to their feet with horror written on their faces. They recoiled at the sight of me, just as my friends had.

My mother's gaze dropped to my dress and the box of roses in my hand before she searched my face. "Belle?" she gasped.

At least she recognized the parts of me that still existed. I burst into tears. "Mama, I've been cursed." I took a step toward them.

My father's hand splayed out in front of him. "Do not come any closer."

He huddled next to my mother, as if my affliction could somehow transmit to him. "We do not want the family curse to fall upon us."

It was my turn to flinch. I retreated to the shadows. My brain was slow to catch on to his words and just as they settled into my brain, I opened my mouth. But my mother's glare at him silenced me.

She peeled herself out of my father's grasp. "What happened?"

"A witch cursed me."

"What did you do to cause that?" Her tone was as harsh as the look she gave me. She always told me to speak with a kind tongue because I could never be certain of the damage I would cause. Tonight, I wished I had heeded her warnings.

My gaze dropped to the ground, and I shifted from foot to foot as heat filled my face. "I was making fun of the way she looked." I wanted to shrink into myself at the admission and the disappointment on my parents' faces.

"And you can't shift one way or the other?" My father's question snapped through the distance like a slap.

I shook my head. "I cannot. She cursed me to remain like this until I find love or the last petal wilts and dies. If I don't find love, I'm stuck like this forever."

"You have got to be kidding me!" My father laughed in his sarcastic way that said so much more than words, and my mother shot him another warning glare, shutting him up.

"I agree with Father," I said. "I don't have a chance at finding love looking like this." I waved my good arm down my form. Before this curse, I could have had anyone I wanted. I had the looks to seduce and manipulate, but now I was a freak that no one could look at without cringing.

"We need to take this to the council and have them force that witch to turn her back!" My mother's voice hit a pitch that hurt my ears, and I whined.

"The witch disappeared," I said, pulling their attention back to where I stood. Although neither of them would look directly at me.

"There has to be a way around this." My mother sounded more desperate than I felt.

My father finally raised his gaze. "You know better than I do just how much our pack detests the abnormal. They will kill Belle," he mumbled as he stared at me. "They will not let something so horrifying live here within our town. I'm surprised they let her leave the ball alive."

I blinked. "Only two of my friends saw me after the witch cursed me. I hid in the bathroom and then snuck out and ran home." My friends had been horrified into silence, and I prayed they'd keep their mouths shut. But I wouldn't bet my life on their silence, not after the spectacle they witnessed.

He huffed and nodded, as if what I said made sense. But I had seen the pack tear a stranger apart for having a stump for a leg. And I had seen them put down the elderly and the sick in the same manner. I shivered. My father was right. Our pack did not allow for anyone or anything that would weaken their status, so I could not rely on my friends to remain silent for long.

"What do I do?"

My parents traded a look.

"There's always my father's estate," my mother whispered.

"But that place hasn't been occupied for years," my father said. "We don't even know if it's still standing."

"It's far enough away that the pack won't kill her." My mother's lips formed a frown. "Pack a bag. We will take you to the estate before judgment can be made here."

She hurried me along to my room, and I threw clothes and treasures into a suitcase and slid the box of roses into a backpack before returning to the front room. My parents were already outside, perched on the bench of the cart they used whenever they went into town to shop for food. A few sacks of grains sat on the back and my father pointed for me to climb up next to the sacks.

Normally, I sat on the bench with them, but the exile to the back was as pronounced as my friends' faces at the ball. I was no longer an accepted member of the pack.

BELLE Chapter 3

THE RIDE WAS LONG and uncomfortable. As the path through the thick woods narrowed to the point the cart could not pass, my father stopped. He hung his head and then glanced back at me.

"You must make your way from here on foot," he said. "I can't set foot on your grandfather's property." He looked away, as if carrying a heavy burden that I had no knowledge of.

My mother balked. "She cannot carry her luggage and the grains herself."

"You know as well as I do that I can't cross onto the estate." He glared at her. "Besides, we cannot leave the horse unguarded in these woods."

"Why not?" I looked between the two of them.

"Bad blood," he said.

It wasn't much of an explanation, but my mother seemed satisfied. She nodded slowly, her frantic gaze calming as some unspoken truth passed between them. "You can stay with the cart. I will help her."

She climbed down before my father could argue and hauled a bag of grains over her shoulder. "We will come back for the last bag," she said to me and started up the path.

I carried my suitcase and my backpack behind her, limping along, with my canine leg and human leg at odds with each other.

"Why can't Dad come up here?" I asked when we were out of earshot.

"He...witnessed...my father's death." Her words were broken, as if she searched for the right words.

"What happened to my grandfather?" The winding path brought us over a hill, and a field stretched out before us. At the far side of the field stood a massive home looming on the top of another hill. It was dark and held a spooky quality that left me cold. A winding, overgrown brick path cut through part of the field, leading to a black gate that encircled the manor.

My mother shivered in front of me at the view and then plodded along to the gate. "He was killed by the pack."

Of all the things that she could have said, what fell from her lips chilled me. No one in town had ever spoken of my grandfather. No one had ever spoken of his death.

We passed through the ominous gates, and the dark magic of this place pressed down on me with a heaviness that almost brought me to my knees.

"What happened here?" I gasped, stumbling behind her, confused by this entire ordeal.

"Nothing good," she mumbled under her breath as her head dipped and her shoulders hunched forward, as if she were plowing through a heavy burden.

"So, why are you forcing me to stay here?"

She pushed the door open and tossed the grain bag inside. Then she held the door open for me to do the same. Her hard stare met mine. "This is the only chance you have to live any sort of life. Now put your things down so you can come back and get the last grain sack."

I stared into the dark and dusty entrance and then back at my mother. "I will never be able to find anyone to love me out here." My voice shook with the despair racking my bones.

"And you will die if you stay with us." She peeled the suitcase out of my hand and tossed it inside, and then did the same with the backpack slung over my shoulder. "I am doing this to prevent you from being killed." She took my cheeks in her hands and forced herself to look in my eyes. "I love you. Despite what this looks like. This is your best chance at survival. And people do come along this way from time to time, so you may have the opportunity to find that someone who can look past this horrid deformity and see into your heart." She grimaced as she spoke. "But you have to be sure your prejudices don't follow you. Making fun of the superficial is a horrid thing to do. Remember that, and learn from your mistakes."

Hot tears choked me, and I nodded, following her back to the path where my father had turned the cart around in our absence.

"If anyone asks who you are, tell them you are a Denton," my father said and glanced at my mother.

She nodded. "That is my family name. Use it to protect yourself and us." She gave me a quick hug and then climbed up onto the cart beside my father.

"For your own good, stay on Denton property." My father nodded toward the house. "If you set foot outside of it, expect to be killed." He glanced at me with his lips pressed together and gave me a resolute nod before snapping the reins. The horses took off.

Leaving me at the side of the path, next to the bag of grains.

I maneuvered it onto my shoulder and started the long trek back to the house. When I closed the door, the cold inside pressed down on me, and I crumpled to the floor as tears continued to run hot paths down my cheeks. The skitter of nails on the floor hitched my breath, and my eyes darted from one dark corner to another. Until I finally saw the three mice that had come out of a crack in the wall. They were just as cautious and wary as I was, but at least there were living things here.

"Hi." I sniffled.

Their little ears perked up and instead of running, they came closer, their little noses twitching with interest. They exchanged a glance and then stared back at me.

"Are you real?" the middle, chunky mouse said in a high, squeaky voice.

Now I squealed and backed up, frightened by the fact the mouse had spoken. They startled as well, but didn't run away like I expected. Instead, they traded another look between the three of them.

"Welcome to the Denton mansion," they said in unison, and bowed their heads. "It has been forever and a day since we have had a visitor." They looked around at the disrepair surrounding them. "We apologize for the sorry state of the house," they added with a lilt of despair in their voices.

I blinked at the rodents. They knew my grandfather's surname and they could speak in full sentences, and they weren't frightened of my deformed physique.

"Who are you?" I whispered, afraid to scare them off.

"We used to be the servants who kept this house in order, but when our master was cursed by a dark witch, the entire estate was cursed. We turned into what you see here. And the curse did not lift when he passed away like we thought it would." The heavy-set mouse sighed.

My eyebrows rose. I had never met my grandfather. My mother told me he passed away before I was born, but after what my parents said tonight, I was starting to believe being cursed ran in my mom's family. "Why was he cursed?"

"He played with the witch's affections, with no thoughts to her feelings, and then dumped her the moment another beauty came along. You see, after his first wife died, his warmth and affection withered until he became a cruel shell of a man. Thankfully, he sent his daughter away after his wife died. He could not stand the sight of her because she reminded him of his wife. If she had stayed..." The mouse shivered. "He would have poisoned her with his bitterness."

So, mean streaks ran in the family, too. What an unsettling thought.

I ran my hand down my face with a sigh. "I am his granddaughter," I said. "And I am cursed for the same type of nastiness." Although perhaps my grandfather's heartbreak of losing his wife was more of a valid excuse than my sudden and irrational need to lash out. It was as if I had been channeling something darker, something tainted. Something as twisted as my grandfather.

Their eyes widened, and they stepped back, studying me. "A shifter stuck in mid-shift." The female mouse gasped. "Just like our master."

"Could it be the same witch?" The heavy mouse chittered and looked me up and down. The three of them nodded, as if the same magic could have claimed me. "She is young. There is hope yet." He glanced at his mates.

"Hope for what?"

"To break the curse."

I laughed and pulled out the rosebush. "I have to find someone to love me before the last petal falls. Otherwise, I will be stuck in this monstrous form."

They stared open-mouthed at the glass case and the full rosebush inside. "Follow us. Bring the rosebush." They ran into the heart of the home, doubling back to ensure I followed.

I lurched forward, carrying the box as I went.

At the end of the hallway at the far side of the dark house, the mice ran under a door, and I swung the door open a moment later. There, in the center of the room, on a pedestal, sat a box similar to mine, with a bare rosebush. The bottom of the box was littered with blackened and withered petals. I shivered and stared at my box with trepidation.

I slowly crossed, trembling from more than the chill in the air. A couple of curtains billowed inward. I slid my box of new flowers next to the one with the dead ones, and the ground seemed to tremble beneath my feet. It seemed that the witch who cursed me, also cursed him. And if history repeated itself, I was doomed to remain in this form until my last breath.

BELLE Chapter 4

IT TOOK ME A good three weeks to clean the mansion from top to bottom until the floors and walls shined with the opulence this place once held. I would not live in squalor and filth. Not when I could still function.

I dropped the mop in the bucket and stared at the grand entry in all its glory. Herman, Faith, and Chauncey stood to the side, grinning in their mouse way at what I had done.

"You have no idea how long we wanted to clean this place." Faith's beady little eyes sparkled.

"I'm not one for living in dirty quarters. My mother taught me to even wipe my paws before I entered her house." I sighed. I missed my parents, and I thought they would be proud of me at how I made this place look shiny and new inside.

The outside was still overgrown and unwieldy, but I'd have to wait until spring to make that presentable. The dark magic still pressed down all around me, but at least with the dust and dirt gone, it didn't seem as overwhelming as the first day I stepped into this deserted mansion.

The only room which I did not touch in my cleaning frenzy was the rose room. I couldn't bring myself to go in there and see how many petals had fallen to fate. Or to view my grandfather's failures so acutely present in his bare rosebush.

Instead, I washed all the rags in the sink and hung them outside the kitchen door to dry. I loaded the hearth with wood and started a fire to get the chill out of the air. Half my body was cold, and the wolf half had no issue with the winter chill layering over the home. Soon, snow would cover the ground and game would be easy to pick out. Of course, my hunting skills left something to be desired in this horrendous form. But I found a spear, along with a bow and arrow set, that, with practice, I could get good at. But for now, it was all more a matter of luck versus skill, and luck had been in my favor when I needed food.

I was sure if I got hungry enough, my mouse family would look like meals, but I'd rather starve than eat any of the mice. Not when they were my only friends.

I made another porridge from the grains my mother had left me and sat at the kitchen counter, eating without tasting. I had to re-learn eating as well due to the mix of human and canine teeth cluttering my disfigured mouth. It wasn't pretty, but it was necessary.

Once I finished and cleaned up the kitchen, I found myself in the extensive library. Now that the shelves were free of dust, the titles filling them called to me. If I couldn't live in the outside world, I would experience it through the words of the authors in these books. I took the first one from the shelf and sat on the window seat.

Movement outside the window caught my eye, and I focused on the outside of the estate, beyond the gates. A person wrapped in rags approached. They had a limp, and dark liquid trailed behind them. Whoever it was, they were injured. I closed the book and darted to the door, swinging it open as the intruder leaned against the gates.

The minute their gaze took me in, their eyes widened, and a high-pitched yelp peeled from their throat. They stumbled backward and landed on their ass. Their hood disengaged, showing off a gaunt face that had no right to judge me. He scrambled backward like a spider, forgetting about his own injury in his bid to get away from the monster in the mansion.

"I can help!" I yelled, but he turned over onto his hands, pushed himself upright, and took off at a limping run. I watched until the woods swallowed him whole.

I thought about following, but the horror and fear on his face had been enough to make me reconsider. If I went after him and he had a weapon, he would likely use it out of fear, and I didn't want to play with fire.

I closed the door and leaned against it, wondering just how I was going to find someone who remained in my company long enough to care about me, never mind fall in love.

As I headed back to my discarded book in the library, despair wrapped an icy hand around my heart.

BELLE Chapter 5

*F*IVE YEARS LATER.

I existed with only the woods and the mice to keep me company. Even the grand library lost its interest after I devoured every book on the shelves at least twice. Even the story of the original royal werewolves and their lost kingdom didn't hold my attention anymore. It was hard to count how many times I read that manuscript and meticulously replaced it after devouring the last word. But that story hit too close to home, with a curse that had to be broken before the royals would once again return to glory.

The rest of the books opened up worlds to me between the covers. Love and loss, battle and victory, sorrow and joy were all outlined within the pages, making me long for a life where I could be the damsel in distress instead of the monster.

With each year that passed, my hope dwindled. As did the rose petals clinging to the vines. Or so the mice told me. I still had not stepped into that room. They informed me that only two roses still bloomed, and Faith said one looked as if it could shed its petals at any moment.

Her voice had been full of the same despair that made my bones ache.

I had had no luck with the other souls that crossed paths with this mansion. Each one reacted similar to that first injured visitor so long ago, screaming or flinching or all but passing out at the sight of me. Some shot curses as to what the hell kind of monster was I, but none broke through the dark magic protecting the mansion from anyone with destructive intent.

I had more than a fleeting viewing with one man who had broken his leg when he fell from his hunting perch. He couldn't run, but he stared at me with horror and revulsion until I finished splinting his leg. I broke a branch for him to use as a crutch and helped him to his feet despite the disgusted frown on his face.

Instead of thanking me, he limped away as fast as humanly possible, without as much as a word.

After that, I only hunted near the mansion. Most nights I went hungry because the animals rarely strayed into the perimeter. I guess the black magic protections freaked them out. Which made sense. My three mice friends would have never survived if this were a haven for wild animals.

Instead of letting myself wallow in pity bend self-disgust, I kept the house clean and worked on the gardens, weeding, pruning, and watering when needed. Now, when I stood at the gates and scanned the landscape in front of the mansion, a well of pride filled me. The house looked like it had in its heyday. At least Herman said so. He had been just as proud as I when I brought them out to see the improvements I had made.

Despite my drawbacks, I had learned to be a homemaker, a decent cook when there was meat to cook, and a gardener with a hell of a green thumb. I wished my mother could see this place now. I thought she would be proud of me, too.

I sat on the front step with a book, letting the sun warm my face. Leaning on the column next to me was my spear. I kept it near in case someone attacked my homestead. I normally had a bow and arrow, but today, I just didn't feel like venturing out into the real world.

The wind blew my hair back from my face, and I swore I heard snarling. I paused, lifting my nose. I concentrated on my wolf sense and what I picked up had my skin prickling. There were shifters out there, and whatever they were hunting reeked of fear.

A pack was hunting on *my* property.

I snarled. I didn't like it when other packs came near my property, even though there could be a mate among them. I usually hid when their scent came my way, especially with the last warnings my parents told me. The pack would kill me if they ever saw me.

But the fear coming from their victim had me moving. It wasn't a rabbit or a deer. It was something just as broken as me, and I couldn't let someone else die because they didn't live up to the pack's expectations. I had a healthy amount of animosity toward the pack at this point. If they were accepting of different, I would have never been exiled to this mansion and this lonely existence.

My book dropped on the step, and I grabbed the spear, moving toward the smells in the wind. I smelled blood as I approached a small clearing in the woods. Pleas of mercy came from a bloody lump on the ground, but the wolves circling him were too lost to the bloodlust of the hunt.

I slammed my spear against the tree as I stepped into the clearing. Although I wanted to make shish kebab of the pack members, I knew they would turn their anger on me.

I thought I recognized one of them, but I wasn't sure. After all, it had been five years since I dropped off the face of the earth. Five years of isolation and learning to survive with my affliction. My only hope was that they did not recognize me.

They jumped back from the man, as if he had been the one to make the noise. I was still upwind from them, but the minute my snarl voiced from my human-wolf throat, they turned in my direction. Four healthy wolf shifters bared their teeth at me and then their eyes widened, as if they beheld an angry ghost.

Fear bloomed in their gazes, not disgust, and certainly not murder.

I pointed the sharp end of the spear at them. "Leave *my property*, now."

The closest one's haunches tightened, as though he were going to launch at me.

"If you want to die, be my guest, but this is my domain." I had enough alpha blood in my family tree to exude that type of vibe. Plus, if the bastard jumped, I would spear his ass and probably die in battle with the other three.

The man's head on the ground came up a fraction, as if he sensed the mercy he had been begging for being granted. He looked in my direction, but his face never scrunched with fear or disgust. It remained a mask of pain.

"Leave!" I stepped farther into the clearing, brandishing my spear. "Or I will gut every one of you!" I put my most feral tone into the words, and they backed off, growling as they passed the figure on the ground. One even went to bite his arm. "Leave him and go," I clarified, taking another step closer.

They backed away, wary of me and the weapon in my hand. I also had my skinning knife hanging from my belt, but they didn't know I couldn't hold it and the spear at the same time. I waited until their scent barely drifted on the wind before I looked down at the injured man.

He had curled up on his side and was shaking. I crouched, laid my weapon on the ground, and touched his shoulder. He jerked.

"It's okay. I'm not going to hurt you."

He turned his head in my direction and, good lord, his face rivaled that of an angel. His blue eyes stared somewhere over my head, but the cringe I expected never came.

"Who are you?" he whispered in a shaky voice.

"Belle Denton. Who are you?"

"Adam Cannon. From Winslow."

"You're a long way from home, Adam. Why was the Averyton pack attacking you?"

He chuckled bitterly. "They don't take too kindly to any shifters that have... physical limitations." He rolled onto his hand and knees, trying to get up, but ended up putting his head onto the ground with a moan.

"What is your ailment?" He looked perfectly fit to me. Broad shoulders, trim waist, thick, powerful thighs, despite the numerous bites and gouges in his skin. He was much more normal than I was.

"I'm blind," he said softly. "Been blind since birth, but my home was overrun by a rival pack hell-bent on destroying us, and those who survived scattered."

His voice was losing strength. I needed to get him back to the mansion so I could patch him up.

Perhaps all it would take was a blind wolf to lift my curse. It was something that five years ago I would never have considered. As a matter of fact, I would have been part of the hunting party. Shame accosted me at the thought, and I handed him my spear.

"Hold this while I help you up. I need to get you out of here before they decide to bring reinforcements."

He took the weapon, and I reached down and slid my arm under his armpit, lifting him to his feet. He cried out in pain, but used the spear in his other hand to steady himself.

For a moment, I almost reconsidered helping him. It would be difficult to feed the two of us with what scraps I had left. But I pushed that thought away. Blind or not, the man needed help, and I had what was needed to dress his wounds in the mansion.

As we made our way through the woods, I caught scents on the wind. Adam stiffened next to me as well.

"There's more of them," he said, and we both picked up our pace.

I knew them leaving was too good to be true. My grandfather's lands hadn't been marked for years, and the lands they were on were on the boundaries, but it still was considered Denton property.

With the mansion in sight, I nearly picked him up and ran, but I wasn't that strong, even with all the physical workouts of upkeeping the house and garden. But I moved faster; so did he, even with his almost constant hiss of pain.

My mind drifted back to the stories of the monster in the woods that the pack hunted down years before I was born. I gasped as the truth barreled through me harder than the magical barrier. My grandfather had been torn to pieces by the pack. Whether he went there with the intention to die or not, he had been in the badlands, where the property lines blended.

I was certain it had to have happened in the same area they were attacking Adam. I even remember traveling to the forbidden woods with some of my friends on a dare. One of them told the story of the monster in the woods that scared everyone who passed by him until one day the elders of the pack slaughtered him.

I blinked at the memory. These parts were off-limits to the pack. We had been told numerous times to steer clear of this area. Most of the pack listened, but there were people like me and my friends taking dares all the time.

As we crossed the field, another truth hit. *Damn. That ghost story was about my grandfather.* I shivered.

When we hit the magical barrier, Adam choked on it, coughing up blood. I almost dropped him on the ground, but I adjusted my grip and yanked him through despite his cry of pain. Then I swung the gate closed behind us, locking it while he sputtered and coughed, covering me with splatters of blood.

"What the hell?" he whispered through the cough.

"Cursed magic." I didn't have time to say more, but I could tell by his stiffening jerk, it wasn't something he expected. Hell, no one expected cursed magic, and I imagined anyone injured would feel it more acutely. I slowed our pace. "We're coming up to the steps." I led him up the stairs and into the grand foyer, where I gently placed him on the floor and left him to retrieve my book. In the distance, I saw the pack breach the woods. I closed the door on the view and focused back on my guest bleeding on the marble entry.

He aimed the tip of the spear in my general direction, although he was off by a couple of feet. If he launched it, the stick would fly harmlessly into the door. "What type of curse?" he gasped, although his coughing and sputtering had stopped now that he was inside the house.

I let a bitter laugh escape. "I don't know. A curse. But it explains why the boys attacking you went to get reinforcements. It wasn't just to finish you off." I tossed the book onto the hall table, the sound making my guest jump.

"What was that?"

"The book I was reading when I got a whiff of the pack spilling blood on my land."

He lowered the spear and laid his head on the floor. "What's the book?" he asked, even though his breathing was thready.

"*The Adventures of Tom Sawyer.* Maybe I'll read a little to you once I get you patched up." *Assuming there's still daylight.* "I'll be right back. I need to get the medical kit." I left him before he could argue and ran down the hall with my heart in my throat.

A terrifying thought scratched at my skin. *The dark magic would keep the pack at bay, wouldn't it?*

Although that was worrisome, the injured blind man on my foyer floor was more pressing. His injuries were serious enough for me to have my doubts, and it wasn't as if I could contact a healer to help. I was on my own.

I prayed the pack wouldn't breach the dark magic and that the stranger wouldn't die on my watch.

BELLE Chapter 6

ADAM HAD FALLEN UNCONSCIOUS during my run for the mending kits, towels, and clean water. I had to tear most of his clothing off to clean and dress his wounds. He was going to have some nasty scars if he survived the blood loss.

Once he was cleaned and the floor mopped of all traces of blood, I stretched out a warm, dry blanket, dragged his clean form onto it, and then pulled it across the foyer into the living room and deposited him in front of the hearth.

I wrapped the blanket around him like he was an infant and started a fire. As soon as the flames were warm enough, I retrieved a pitcher of water, a pot, and a couple of glasses, along with the vegetables I had left. I poured water into the pot and dumped the vegetables in. A vegetable broth was the best I could do, and Adam would need something to gain strength once he woke.

If he woke.

I swept that thought away as I hung the pot over the fire and took a seat on the couch. When I brought a glass to my lips, that was when I saw the tremble in my hand. I had gone on autopilot the moment I stepped into that clearing and now the entire afternoon had me shaking. I glanced down at my clothing and closed my eyes. I was covered in blood and needed to wash it off before I ended up throwing up the water I just ingested.

I pulled the pot away from the fire. All I needed was to burn the only food in the house while I cleaned up. Then I went and filled the tub upstairs. Plunging into the cold water, I scrubbed my skin and fur clean before I stepped out and found another outfit to put on. The bloody clothing would end up in the fire because they were too soiled to have a prayer of getting the stains out.

I stopped at my grandfather's armoire and opened it. I might need to tailor some of his clothing if mine kept getting ruined. But he had shelves upon shelves of trousers and shirts. They were big enough that I thought they'd fit Adam, and I brought an outfit down for him for when he woke up.

By the time I returned, the pot was steaming. It would boil in no time once I put it back over the fire. I added more water and left it in place, checking on my unconscious guest.

His slack features warmed me more than the fire. I checked his pulse, and it was stronger than it had been earlier.

I went into the hallway, retrieved my book, and settled myself on the floor between the fire and Adam, where I'd have more light.

Licking my lips, I cracked open my book and began reading Mark Twain's *Tom Sawyer* out loud, only pausing to add more logs to the fire when the flames died down.

My mice came out from the hole and lined up at Adam's feet.

"Who is this?" they asked in unison.

"Adam. The pack attacked him near our border, so I saved him and brought him here to heal." I found my place in the book again and focused on the words, resuming reading out loud.

"He didn't run when he saw you?" they asked. They were as used to the reaction to me as I was at this point.

"He's blind," I said between words and continued the story.

Their little mouths hung open, but their eyes sparkled with the possibilities. I glared at them over the book and shooed them away with my paw, seeing as my hand was holding the book open.

I had learned to do a lot of things with only one hand over the last five years. I was blissfully self-sufficient, something I did not think possible when I first set foot in this house. The only thing I lacked confidence in was the belief that anyone, blind or not, would find me attractive enough to fall in love with, and I did not want to see the hope rise in the mice eyes staring back at me, as if their curse could somehow be lifted before the last petal fell.

BELLE Chapter 7

THE FOLLOWING AFTERNOON, ADAM still remained unconscious, but at least he wasn't feverish anymore. It had been quite the night, feeding the fire continuously and re-covering him every time he had gone through night sweats, from throwing the blanket away from him to teeth-chattering shivers.

I continued to feed the fire even though the afternoon sun warmed the room through the windows.

During the night, the pack disbanded and I couldn't catch a whiff of them when I stepped out to cool off. I guess with nothing to see and no way to breach the barrier of dark magic; they decided killing us wasn't worth waiting us out.

I picked up my book again and cleared my throat, starting up on a new chapter of *Tom Sawyer*. Every other sentence, my gaze drifted to Adam's bare chest, and then I'd have to find where I left off. The stilted reading was enough to annoy me, but my unconscious guest didn't seem to mind.

It was right about the scene where Tom and his friend Huckleberry were in the cemetery that a noise sounded from below me, and I jumped. My gaze darted to Adam. He had rolled onto his side and propped his head on his folded hands.

"Don't stop," he said in a groggy, shallow voice.

"I have a pot of vegetable broth." I ignored his plea.

"Not yet. I was enjoying your reading." He looked in my general direction. "Your voice is soothing, despite the tension in the scene you're reading."

I laughed a little. *My growling, half-human, half-wolf voice was soothing? It takes all kinds.* I found where I had left off and began again, but now that I had Adam's rapt attention, it was more difficult to concentrate on the book rather than make sure he was comfortable. Although shifters healed quicker than humans, the sheer number of injuries he had sustained wasn't going to be all better overnight.

I finished the chapter, folded the corner of the page, and closed the book. "It's time to eat." I left no leeway in my decree.

And Adam didn't argue. He sat up slowly, wincing a little. The blankets fell around his waist, giving me a full view of him. His fingers inspected a few of the patches on his chest and arms.

I grabbed the empty bowl off the table near me, along with a spoon, and poured him a ladle of the vegetable broth with some vegetables. "It isn't much." I handed him the bowl. "And here's a spoon," I added after he took the bowl from my hand.

"This is more than I've had in a while." He took a spoonful, blew on it, and dipped it into his mouth as if it were the most heavenly thing he'd ever had.

"Funny, you don't look like you're starving," I mumbled at the muscle definition. But then I noticed the outline of his ribs were a little more pronounced on his sides now that he sat up.

He snorted a laugh. "I used to be quite a bit bigger. Enough so assholes like those who attacked me would think twice about it."

"Mmm. I don't think your size would have mattered." I glanced at the front window. "The Averyton pack seeks perfection. Anyone imperfect is a target." I knew that fact all too well. It was what got me in this predicament. Although, being on this side of things had me reconsidering their entire philosophy. "If I had stayed after I was cursed, I would have been ripped to shreds."

He tipped the bowl to his lips, finishing the rest before he put it down on the floor at his side.

"Do you want more?"

He pressed his lips together and felt around for the bowl. "As long as there is enough," he said, as if he were familiar with lean times.

I glanced in the pot. "Well, if we want anything for dinner, we might want to hold off." I sighed. "I haven't been hunting in a few days and that magical barrier I pulled you through kind of discourages animals within the grounds."

"I thought I smelled mice." He sniffed the air.

"We can't have the mice," I replied quickly, and his eyebrows shot up.

"A vegetarian wolf? Is that your curse?"

I laughed in my snorting way. "No. God, no. The mice are my grandfather's servants. When he was cursed, apparently, they were too, in a different manner of speaking. So, no, we will not be eating the mice inside this house. However, if I find field mice out in the woods, that is a very different situation."

His blind eyes went wide, and his mouth dropped open slowly as my words sunk in. "Are you...a mouse?" His voice squeaked as he asked the question.

Oh my, that tickled my funny bone, and I laughed like I hadn't in years. Many more years than just the five relegated to this house. "No," I managed to say, but the thought of it just dropped me into the land of insane giggles.

His lips eventually twitched into a smile, and he put the bowl out in his outstretched hand, a few feet away from where I sat. "Save this for later," he said through his own chuckle. "And

I guess that really was a stupid question to ask."

"No, no, it wasn't." My laughter finally sputtered out, but not before my human face was coated with hot tears of mirth. "I have not laughed like that in years." I took his bowl from him, setting it by mine. "Thank you."

"No. It's me who should thank you." He waved at the patch jobs across his chest.

"Speaking of your injuries, I should redress your wounds. Many of those bandages are sweat soaked from your fever." I pulled open the cabinet under the table next to me where I had stowed the medical supplies the prior night and pulled out the bandages and the bowl I had used to clean his wounds. I added water from the pitcher into a bowl so that I could dip a clean cloth in to wash his wounds again.

"I should be fine," Adam said as I set things down next to him.

I snorted a laugh. "Well, I would rather not have to deal with infection, if you don't mind." I moved closer to him and reached for the first bandage, tugging at it.

His hand came up and covered mine, stopping me.

"Really. You don't need to waste your supplies on me."

I studied his face and then moved his hand away. "I have enough medical supplies to patch up an army," I said, stretching the truth. I could replace his patches maybe one more time after this and then my supplies would be exhausted.

The way his lips tilted into a smile caught me off guard, and I took a heavy breath, tugging at the dressing of the one I had started on before. The adhesive pulled at his skin, and he winced. I hesitated and wished I had two hands.

My gaze fell to his. *Duh. I've got three hands at my disposal.*

"I may need your help." I reached for his far hand, placing it on the skin near the edge of the bandage. "Keep your skin stretched a little while I try to get the bandage off, okay?"

He nodded but said nothing, steeling himself as I peeled the patch off again. This time, it came easier with his help.

"Thank you," I said after the first bandage was discarded.

His hand dropped and brushed along my wolf fur. He jolted and his eyebrows rose, but he didn't ask the questions running across his features. I waited for disgust to crawl over the surprised look, but it never came. He just waited patiently for me to continue.

I dipped the cloth into the cool water, squeezing out as much of the water that my fist would allow, and then I blotted the skin around the cut gently.

Adam closed his eyes and laid his head back against the couch. "Tell me about your curse," he whispered with a voice that echoed the grimace on his lips as I continued to clean out his wound.

This gash looked uncomfortable, but at least it didn't have red outlining the cut. It actually looked as if it were healing quite nicely. Still, I covered it once I got all the crusty blood wiped away.

"It's a vanity curse," I said. "I guess so I'd learn a valuable lesson." I huffed and tugged at the next bandage. "Although I'm not sure what the lesson is, especially since my pack wants me dead in this form."

His head popped up and his blind gaze widened.

How could eyes be so damn expressive without sight?

"Your pack?" His hand gripped my wrist, this time with a little more force than before. He pushed me away.

I nodded, and tears sprouted at the hard lines, making his face tragic and beautiful.

"Was that your pack that attacked me?" A dark tone bled into his words.

I realized he hadn't seen me nod. "Yes. That had been my pack before I was cursed."

He shifted farther away from me and ran his fingers over the clean patch. "I don't understand," he finally said. "There wasn't a single redeeming member of that pack."

"Yeah. They are militant in their ways. And if you saw me, you'd probably want me dead, too."

He let out a sharp, angry laugh. "It doesn't matter what you look like. I would never wish you harm for an ailment you are helpless against. It's inhuman."

His venom brought forth a wave of pure shame.

"If you hadn't been cursed, would you have joined them in trying to kill me?"

His question jolted me, and I slid back out of his reach. It wasn't an easy question to answer, and I mulled it over. *Would I have joined in to murder another werewolf just because they were different?*

Sure, I made fun of people who were not in the same circles that I kept, but did that equate to bloodlust?

"Well?" His face reddened at my silence.

"I don't know. Had I not been here learning to be self-sufficient with my own disabilities?" I shook my head, ran a hand down my face, and let out a loud sigh. "Had I been at home with the pack's slanted thought process poisoning my brain the last five years, I probably would have been part of the hunting crew," I finally admitted, even though it burned.

"I shouldn't be here." He started to get up, but his legs, which had taken more bites than his torso, couldn't hold his weight yet. He slumped back down to the ground.

"You can't go just yet. I think the pack has sentries watching the house. I caught wind of them when I went to get some more wood. And I wouldn't put it past them to have the perimeter patrolled, either. They don't take kindly to being bested by a monster."

His brow creased as he looked in my general direction. But I wasn't going to expand on the fact that the same pack killed my grandfather for the same ailments that afflicted me.

"Now, are you going to let me refresh the rest of your bandages?" I asked softly.

He closed his eyes and hung his head. "Fine." Although, with his tone, everything was not fine. It was as if I became his mortal enemy the moment I admitted to being one of the pack that attacked him. I guess if I were in his position, I probably would be in the same frame of mind. I all but admitted if I hadn't been cursed, I would have been a murderer.

I slid the bandages, cloth, and water closer and began removing, cleaning, and replacing all the bandages on his body. After, Adam lay on his stomach on the blanket, with his chin propped in his fists.

I threw all the soiled bandages in the fire. The flames licked at the new energy source, flaring as it greedily devoured the cloth.

"You really would have been party to that?" he asked after a long period of silence.

"I wasn't very nice," I admitted. "I have clothes for you if you'd like," I added at his scowl.

His forehead creased. "You are just full of contradictions." He pushed himself into a sitting position. "You tell me you weren't a nice person. Then you show me just what kind of person you truly are by bandaging me up and offering me clothing to replace the ones ruined by a pack you say you are a part of." He shook his head. "You make no sense."

I sighed. I knew I contradicted all that I had been raised to believe. This curse opened my eyes to the extent of poisonous thoughts I had lived with daily. The quest for perfection in the mirror overrode the pursuit of kindness.

"Would you like some clothes? They were my grandfather's, and I think they'll fit," I said, because he hadn't answered my question.

Adam nodded. "That would be nice. I'm sure it has to be a bit unsettling for you to see a near-naked man lounging on your floor."

"I would think it is more unsettling for you." I stood and retrieved my grandfather's clothes that I had brought down, and handed them to him. "Here. I hope they fit."

"I'm sure they'll be just fine." He pulled on the clothing. The trousers fit him comfortably, but the shirt was just a little too small for him to button. Although it fit the expanse of his shoulders without ripping.

I would have to let out some seams to give him the room he needed in the next pair I offered him. Assuming there would be another pair, given where our conversation had led.

"You don't want that too tight against your cuts. Leave it unbuttoned," I said as he struggled to bring the button to the hole. I can't say

I was upset because it wasn't as if he sported a beer belly, like some guys in town. He was extremely easy on the eyes, and I was both relieved that he was mostly covered and a little disappointed because he was so pleasant to look at. My cheeks heated at the thought, and I mentally scolded myself for the inappropriate and shallow response. That was something I would have thought before the curse.

He gave up. "Think you could give me a hand onto this couch? It might be a little more comfortable than the floor."

"Sure. If you don't mind being touched by a bona fide freak," I said, trying to lighten the mood.

His blind gaze traveled in my direction. "I don't mind if you don't mind."

Oh. He was so not a freak. Those words almost popped out of my mouth, but I clamped my lips tight on them and shuffled over, bending down so my human arm could sling under his shoulder.

"Ready?" I asked, mindful of his leg injuries. The one on his right thigh was still the most tender of the wounds.

"Yes." He tightened his jaw and used his right arm to gain leverage on the couch. "On three."

"One, two, three," I counted and on three, I hauled him up to the couch.

He winced and then shuffled himself back until he seemed comfortable. But a light sheen of sweat formed on his forehead and the smile he sent as a thank-you looked about as strained as they come. The couch itself wouldn't fit his outstretched body, but he could lay on his side with his knees bent.

"Marginally better," he said.

"You're welcome to stretch out on your side if it's more comfortable. There are pillows at each end that you can prop your head on."

"See, you are nicer than you think you are," he said, and this time a more natural smile appeared as he did as I offered. "I promise, I'm not usually as needy as this," he said after he situated himself. "Do you mind reading some more?"

"Not at all." And I launched into the last half of *Tom Sawyer* until the sun went down and the fire nearly sputtered out.

BELLE Chapter 8

DINNER CONSISTED OF THE rest of the soup in the pot. After I finished, I brought the pot and the bowls into the kitchen, and set about scrubbing them clean before putting them away. Then I looked at the pantry to make sure I had missed nothing. The cupboards were bare.

There was no food anywhere. No grains, no vegetables, and certainly no meat. Which meant I'd have to go out hunting. With the sentries posted near my lands. The thought of that made me shiver. They knew I existed and would attack on sight. I didn't have much for defenses either.

Damn. Was this the same choice my grandfather had to make?

I came back into the living room and curled up in my chair, staring at the fire as my nerves piped in and make my skin feel like ants, or worse, spiders, were marching over my body. I shuddered at the thought of going outside.

"Everything okay?" Adam asked.

"No." I sighed. "We just finished the last of what my garden produced, and I need to go hunting."

His brow furrowed with worry. "They are still out there, aren't they?"

I said nothing. I was sure they were there, just waiting for one of us to venture out. It was problematic. If I harmed a pack member, even in defense, they would be relentless.

"Belle?"

"Yes. They are out there. If I don't go, we will starve to death, and you need actual food to heal."

"And what happens if they attack you?" he asked calmly, but the shake in his voice outed his nerves. "I can go a day or two without food," he said, as if that settled the issue.

"And then we still have the same problem, but we'll be desperate enough not to use caution and walk right into an ambush." As much as I did not want to go out, waiting would make it that much more difficult.

He covered his face with his hand. "I feel useless."

"Injured isn't useless." Although it made it difficult. I would prefer someone out there to have my back, but he wasn't in any condition to fight off the pack if they attacked. Neither of us were. I didn't have the luxury of shifting and he couldn't put pressure on his right leg yet.

"You really have lost your grip on reality." He laughed in a way that wasn't all that flattering.

My defenses went up at his tone. "What is that supposed to mean?"

"Injured *is* useless. I can't put weight on my leg. I can't get out of your hair and take my chances out there in this condition. And I can't hunt with you." Adam waved at his leg in disgust.

"You hunt?" It spilled out before I could catch it.

"I'm blind, not incapable." His tone cooled as he turned his head toward me. "Sure, I run into a tree now and then, but what's a little concussion when you get to take down that deer?"

I blinked at him and then my lips formed into a smirk. I didn't want to laugh at the image that played in my mind. When his dimples appeared and he glanced away, I caught his attempt at humor.

"You do not run into trees." I didn't pose it as a question.

"No. Not anymore, but I did a lot as a pup. I learned to smell the difference between the open air and a tree blocking my path. And if I'm running, my pant sounds different when a tree is approaching."

I had never thought of those things. "I hope I get to see that someday."

His eyebrows arched. "You want to see me hit a tree?"

I snorted a laugh. "No, silly. I want to see you hunt someday."

He smiled at my laughter and then it faded into a serious expression that looked almost as if it had crawled into the land of longing. "I hope like hell I will get to hunt again."

I hoped so too. But it would be another few days of healing before he could try to put pressure on it without the fear of it breaking open again. I was amazed that the pack had hit nothing vital in their attack. It was as if they were toying with him for the sheer joy of basking in his fear. The thought set my teeth on edge.

"The chunk they took out of the back of your thigh is going to take time to heal. And you need protein to help with that. You're also going to need your strength for some serious physical therapy to get back to hunting shape. Everything else is superficial in comparison. And you aren't out of the woods yet for infection. That is the one that still needs the dressing changed daily."

He nodded, although he didn't look pleased. "Do you have yarrow growing in the yard?"

"Yes. In the back. Why?"

"Yarrow paste has infection-fighting properties."

"And how does one make yarrow paste?" I didn't know, and although I had been here a good amount of time on my own, I still had a lot to learn about survival.

"The leaves of the flower and a little water in a mortar and grind it into a paste with a pestle." He lifted an eyebrow at me. "Didn't you learn about healing herbs?"

"No. I was taught what was poisonous, though." Even with Herman, Faith, and Chauncey trying to educate me the best that they could on what I could and couldn't eat, they never broached the subject of healing herbs.

"At least you weren't total heathens," he teased. "Go get me some of those flowers and the tools, and I'll teach you how to make the paste. Then we'll discuss hunting again."

Just the way he said it made me think he was going to try to dissuade me from hunting for game. If I had to, I'd go out once he was asleep because the man needed real food, not just vegetable-flavored water.

BELLE Chapter 9

I VENTURED OUT TO the back of the estate with a kitchen bucket and picked what I could of the yarrow between the layers of fallen leaves. At least snow hadn't fallen yet, and it was easy to find the small white flowers that still bloomed. The ground moved ahead of me, and I instinctively pounced, dropping the bucket. For the first time in months, an animal—or reptile, in this case—crossed my property within the magical barrier.

The problem with pouncing on the tail end of a snake was that the head could still strike. I had a hiss as a warning, and I reached my hand out, catching the fangs in the meat of my palm instead of my cheek, where it had aimed. I snapped my teeth on the snake's neck, severing its head from the rest of its body before it could dislodge and slither away. There was no way I was losing this meal.

It took a second for the pain to register, and I grumbled at the head still stuck in my palm as the burn of the venom slowly spread through my hand.

"Damn it," I snarled. I picked up the bucket and the rest of the dead snake and headed inside as fast as I could. I needed the venom out, now. If I lost this hand, I would not survive.

"Adam?" I stumbled into the living room, setting the bucket and the snake on the floor near my chair as I tried not to let the rising panic cloud my mind.

He turned toward my voice, his face a mask of worry. "What's wrong?"

I stared at the snake embedded in my palm and thought of a delicate way to say that I was hurt. He might never let me leave this house at this rate, judging by the fear present in his blind eyes. "I need your help. I seem to have a snake attached to my hand."

He blinked rapidly, as if he were processing my words. "Is it poisonous?"

"It's a copperhead. A pretty good size one, too, so it will make a decent meal or two"—*or a dozen, if we're cautious*—"for us."

His shoulders relaxed. "Did you get the yarrow?"

"Yes." I still stared at the enormous head in my hand and the redness creeping across my palm as the poison spread.

"Okay, then try not to move quickly, but I need you to bring me some soap, some water, and the tools to grind the petals to make the paste, along with a couple of clean rags. If you can do all that by keeping your hand lower than your heart, that would be good. I'll clean your wound and use some of the yarrow paste on it as well."

His calm tone made my pounding heart slow a little and controlled the rising fear. "I won't lose my hand?"

Adam laughed. "No. Belle. It's not like it was a rattlesnake. If that had been the case, I wouldn't be so calm."

This time his laughter didn't trigger my defenses like his earlier cackle had. This was a genuine laugh, one full of mirth and promise, and it warmed my heart. Either that or the poison was affecting me oddly.

I trudged to the kitchen and bathroom, retrieving the items in a dry bucket and one that I filled halfway with water. I pressed the dry bucket of things against my body and carried the water in my swelling hand.

When I returned, I dumped the dry bucket in the center of the table and nested the buckets together to the side of the messy pile of stuff.

"I brought some towels, along with clean rags," I said.

Adam had moved himself into the corner near the table. A light sweat stood out on his forehead, as if the movement had taxed him more than he would ever admit. When I sat beside him, he put both hands out. I placed my hand palm facing the ceiling into his.

"The snake is still...embedded." I winced as he took hold of my hand and traced my palm with the fingers of his free hand.

"I see." He felt the outline and where the teeth still penetrated the meat of my thumb. He cocked his head. "This is a rather large snake." He gripped the sides of the snake's head and yanked upward without warning.

I hissed through my teeth as the pain of it ripping loose surpassed the discomfort of the poison in my hand.

"Soap and a wet cloth, please." He dropped the snake's head on the floor and held his hand out. I went to pull my human hand away, but he gripped it tighter. "Don't move this hand."

"I can't get the soap and a wet cloth with a wolf paw." He might as well understand my limits and my curse. "I am partially shifted. That's what the witch did to me. I don't have two hands like you."

"Fine. Where did you put everything?" His voice was clipped with impatience.

"On the table behind you."

He turned, wincing, and slowly felt along the tabletop. His hand landed on the pile of rags and towels. He pulled one from the pile and felt until he came to the bucket. He dropped the rag in.

"The soap is next to the rags. It may even be under them."

When he found the soap, he pulled the wet rag from the water, squeezed some of the water out, but it still dripped as he turned back toward me. He put the soap on his thigh and gently wiped the cloth from the center of my hand outward.

I watched in fascination as he accurately ran the cloth over the teeth marks, as though he could truly see. He traded the towel for the soap and lathered up my hand before he wiped it clean with the wet cloth. I didn't dare tell him there was still soap near my pinkie when he finished, either. He dropped the wet cloth on the floor, where it landed on the discarded snake head. Then he set the soap on the table and took a clean rag, loosely tying it around my hand.

"Now get me the stuff to make the paste and keep your hand as low as possible." His words were stern, but not harsh.

I retrieved the bucket of yarrow, the mortar, and the pestle, along with the half-full pitcher I used for our drinking and cooking water. It took me longer than normal because I was retrieving things one at a time and handing them to him. When I handed him the water pitcher, he settled that between his legs and got to work.

I sat on the couch, watching Adam pluck the delicate petals off the flowers. When he had a dozen of them in the mortar, he dipped his fingers into the pitcher and let droplets slide into the mortar. He put six drops of water in with the petals and then handed me the pitcher. I put it on the table behind me without turning away. He ground with the pestle, stopping every so often to test the mixture with his fingers.

My hand throbbed just watching him, but he fascinated me enough to almost forget about my injury.

He finally stopped grinding and set the pestle on the table behind him. "Give me your hand."

I put my hand on top of his, and he unwrapped the rag before he smeared yarrow paste all over the heel of my thumb, covering the bites on the first try.

"Did I cover the bites?"

His question brought a smile to my face. "You did. For someone who's blind, you're pretty accurate."

His lips quirked into a hint of a smile at my incredulous tone.

The bites prickled, as if my palm were a little too close to a fire. "Is it supposed to tingle?"

He nodded as he wrapped my hand a little tighter this time. "Yes. That's how you know it's working." He leaned back and handed me the mortar. "I think maybe I'm going to need some of that on my leg, sooner rather than later."

My gaze shot from my hand to his pale face. I'd been so focused on the action of his hands that I didn't catch what his movements were doing to him.

"And I think I may need to lie on the floor for this," he added.

"Let me move the things you threw down here. I'd hate for you to step on the snake by accident." I cleared the space and straightened out the blankets on the floor, giving him a little more padding this time. The rest of the snake I hung near the hearth; I'd skin and cook that as soon as I finished tending to his wound. "There. I tried to make it a little softer this time."

He slid down onto the blankets and unbuckled his pants, stripping and setting them aside as he stretched out on his stomach. I moved the pillow with my foot until he felt it and wrapped his arms around it, settling his cheek on it as he faced the warmth of the fire.

I set the mortar down and concentrated on peeling the largest bandage off the back of his leg. This gouge was the worst of them and right now, the edges were an angry red.

"Put this on the entire cut?" I stared at it. I really should clean it, but I didn't know whether that would compromise the yarrow paste on my palm or not.

"Yes. As thick as you can get it."

I scooped the paste onto my fingers and gently ran them over the length of the cut, covering the wound—along with the reddened skin at the edges—with the yarrow. He hissed between his teeth when I touched the reddest parts.

"It's a wonder they didn't hit anything vital," I marveled as I wiped my fingers on the wet cloth he had discarded. If they had hit an artery, he would have died before I got him through the front gate. "I don't think I should re-bandage it yet."

He looked in my general direction. "Is that just because you like the view?" His lips tilted in a smile.

I snorted a laugh but found my eyes moving to his round butt cheeks. The view was certainly not bad, and I had to clench my hand to stanch the sudden urge to run my fingers over his ass. "No. It's not just because I like the view." Heat filled my face. "What I mean is, I think it will heal better by getting some air rather than being bandaged."

"Mhm." He smiled and put his head down again.

Now I wanted to swat his ass. "Seriously, I think your pants rubbing against the dressing irritated it some."

His smile faded, and he lifted his head to look in my general direction. "How so?"

"It's red around the edges. None of your other injuries have taken on that angry-looking quality." It wasn't to where red veins were coming from the wound. That was the kind of infection I was afraid to discover on him, because it usually was a death sentence without the proper medicine.

"Then it's a damn good thing you have yarrow outside." He laid his cheek back on the pillow. "You might want to throw that snake head in the fire so neither one of us step on it."

I picked up the head and tossed it into the fireplace, where it landed in the crossbars of the wood and immediately ignited.

"That smells good," he mumbled.

He wasn't the only one with a watering mouth. That smelled divine, and I glanced at the rest of the snake. "Give me an hour, and I'll have a plateful of snake meat cooked up for us."

"You really shouldn't be using your hand so much." He glanced in my direction. "Seriously, you should be resting."

"Yeah, well, we both need food, and that flaming snake head is making my stomach thunder like I haven't eaten in months. Besides, we don't want the meat to go bad." It would only take a little while and my stomach rumbled, making my point painfully known.

"Fine. Just don't...just take it easy. Okay?"

I covered most of him with the throw blanket from the back of my chair, leaving his leg with the yarrow paste uncovered, and then I attended to skinning and cooking the snake.

BELLE Chapter 10

ADAM FELL INTO A restless sleep while I prepared the snake. It took me longer because of my hand, but with my wolf appendage, it was easier to gut and clean out. The guts and skin went into the fire, adding to the succulent scent filling the house.

As soon as I put the snake on the spit and placed it over the flames, I took another look at Adam's leg. The yarrow paste seemed to work. The wound wasn't as inflamed as it had been when I put the paste on. I entertained going out and getting more flowers to crush in case he needed more, but I'd probably burn the snake. Besides, exhaustion was taking its toll, making my eyelids heavy.

In the interest of our meal, I stood and tended to it instead of relaxing in my chair, where I'd likely fall asleep and ruin the only meal we were going to get until I was well enough to hunt again. My getting bitten was just par for the course, but scoring the snake had been a true stroke of luck.

Maybe my bad luck streak was finally through with me.

I had gotten used to this form and survived despite what the witch did. I never lamented over how many rose petals were left, and I wasn't sure whether that was my brain's way of buffering me from major disappointment or getting me to accept what I was. I had resigned myself to be in this form until I died.

But with Adam lying on my floor—granted, he was only here because he was injured—I dared to think of the possibilities. Maybe there was a chance for love, despite my hideous form.

I shook the thought right out of my head as Herman, Faith, and Chauncey came out of the wall, sniffing at Adam as they passed him to come near to me.

Faith pointed her little paw toward the fire. "You'll want to turn those soon," she said in her squeaky voice.

Adam's eyes opened and his head lifted. "Did you say something?" He looked in the general direction of where the mice were.

"No." I glanced at the meat. Faith was right, and I turned the spit so the snake wouldn't burn. She nodded her little mouse head at me.

His head turned toward me. "Then who just spoke?"

"Um. One of the mice." I refocused on him.

His eyebrows arched.

"You told him about us?" Herman looked every bit as annoyed as his voice conveyed.

"He wanted to eat you. So, yes. I told him about you and that we do not eat mice that are in the house." A part of me realized how insane this conversation sounded out loud. In the real world, mice didn't talk.

Adam ran a hand through his hair, leaving it in a spiked mess. "You might want to check my thigh, because I'm not sure if I'm hallucinating."

"You're not," I said at the same time as all three mice.

He cupped his chin in his fist as he settled back on the pillow with his eyebrows held low in contemplation. "Talking mice?" he finally asked and cocked his head.

"We aren't really mice. We were afflicted along with this entire manor when Belle's grandfather was cursed. And this is what became of us." Faith sighed. "There was one more of us in the beginning—Joe, the stable master. But he got stuck outside and froze to death."

"You never told me that." I stared at the mice.

"Why was her grandfather cursed?" Adam asked after a moment.

Herman cleared his throat. "After Belle's grandmother passed, Henry never recovered. He had the sense to send his only child away before he poisoned her innocence. Without her to temper him, he became truly vicious, and most of the servants fled from his wrath. One day a pretty young lady happened upon the manor. He took advantage of her and then threw her out the door after he had claimed what he wanted. Unfortunately, he violated a witch, and she cursed him the same way she cursed Belle. I wouldn't doubt that ancient thing was still walking about, pulling the wool over people's eyes. I think she did it on purpose. She sought the nastiest person in the region and then cursed them."

I made a cutting motion across my throat at the mice. I did not want them to tell Adam the rest. I didn't want him to think I had an ulterior motive for saving him.

But Adam was a smart wolf. "To what end?" he asked, his brow creased in concentration. "For a witch to curse someone, they had to have a good reason and a purpose. Otherwise, they are just as bad as those they are cursing."

He had a point and one that I wouldn't have been able to answer a week ago. At least not with the conviction I had now.

"I think she wanted to teach me a lesson. One I have learned many times over since," I replied.

"What point is that?" He glanced in my direction, but was a few feet off.

"That kindness should be our first instinct, not ridicule. Love should be our knee-jerk reaction, not hate." I took a breath and tended to our meal. "My grandfather never learned that." I tested the piece of meat, and it tasted divine.

"Here, try this." I put the other half of the piece I tested near Adam's mouth.

He opened his mouth, and I popped the piece onto his tongue. He chewed it slowly and closed his eyes. "Just as good as fresh venison." He smiled and his eyes opened.

I slid the snake off the spike, put half of the meat on one plate, and set it down in front of Adam. "I hope this is enough," I said as I moved his hand to the dish so he could eat.

I took the rest and headed toward my chair.

"Aren't you going to eat with me?" Adam patted the blanket. "An indoor picnic?"

The mice all looked at one another and scurried off, leaving me to deal with Adam's half-smile that made my knees wobble.

"Sure." I rerouted to the spot next to him on the floor.

He rolled onto his side, facing me, and moved his plate in front of him. He propped himself up on his hand and sighed. "How's your hand?" he asked as his fingers inspected the plate. The crease between his eyes deepened. "Did you take any for yourself?"

"Yes," I said through a mouthful and then swallowed it down. "It was an enormous snake, and that's half of it." My gaze moved to where the blanket just barely covered him. Rolling the way he had exposed enough of his leg and ass to make the room feel ten degrees warmer.

He nodded and, to my disappointment, moved the blanket over himself a little more. "Just making sure because there's a lot here." He dug into the first piece as if it were a finer meal than it really was. "And it is cooked to perfection," he said after he swallowed. He had the good manners not to talk with his mouth full.

I only could eat a few pieces before I pushed the plate aside. I grabbed another pillow off the couch and threw it on the ground near Adam. "I can't finish mine," I mumbled and stretched out with my back to the fire. "And I can't seem to keep my eyes open." I yawned out the words.

My eyes closed.

"Belle?" Concern laced his voice, but I was already falling into the black of night.

BELLE Chapter 11

HANDS SHOOK ME IN the dark. A chill layered over me and my teeth chattered. A voice whispered in my ear like an early spring wind before a storm, warming the chill from my bones. *Belle, you need to wake up.*

Heat wrapped around me like a vise, holding my legs straight and my arms to my side. I tried to struggle against whatever was holding me still.

"Belle, stop struggling. I am not going to hurt you," a voice barreled in my ear.

My eyes shot open to the cold fireplace. Adam had his arm wrapped around me and his uninjured leg thrown over my legs, keeping mine to the floor. He held my wrist tight enough for my hand to tingle and had my hand on the floor.

"What the hell?" I hissed.

"Just be still and take slow breaths until your head clears."

"Why?"

"Snake poison. You did too much after being bitten." His stressed voice told me more than I really wanted to know.

I slowly relaxed into him. "I'm sorry," I whispered.

His low chuckle tickled my ear, and he rested his forehead on the back of my shoulder. "You scared me." He sighed. "I wasn't sure what the hell to do when your breathing turned to labored wheezing."

My gaze landed on the fireplace again. "How long have I been delirious?" That fire had been blazing hot when we sat down to eat, and now it was reduced to ash.

"Hours."

"And you've been holding me like this that whole time?" I glanced over my shoulder at him. He raised his head from my shoulder and laid it back on the couch right behind him. At least he had chosen a place where he had back support.

"Not the entire time, but most of it when your mice friends said to keep you as still as possible until you woke." He licked his lips. "They calmed me a little. They said you were strong and would survive this, but in order to not make it worse, they insisted I hold you in a sitting position with your snake bite lower than your heart." He still held my hand lower than the rest of me.

"You think there still is poison in my hand?"

His hand relaxed around my wrist, but he didn't remove it. "Probably not, but just keep it there for now." He straightened his leg out, placing it by mine, but the movement pulled a wince.

"How are you doing?" Worry laced my voice.

"I'm doing better," he said, but he didn't sound it. Adam shook his leg and moved his toes. "My leg fell asleep."

"That is the worst," I said, as he continued to stretch and flex his bare leg. "But how is the other leg doing?" I clarified.

"It actually feels a lot better, despite not getting much rest. But I ate a lot of the snake pieces you left on your plate." He sounded as if he regretted taking my food.

I still wasn't hungry, but he had left enough to satiate me when my hunger returned.

"That's okay. You need it more than I do."

He lowered his arm that he had across my chest and rested it on my thigh. "I am going to need to get a little rest."

I started to move, and that arm slung across me.

"Don't move until I wake up. Okay?"

"But the fire." I waved my paw toward the fireplace.

"Look, until I'm certain you are okay, you are not moving. And tending to a fire is the last thing you should do right now. What part of stay still for a while did you not understand?" A little bite of irritation slipped into his voice. He took a deep breath. His fingers trailed over my chest as he moved his hand from holding onto me. When his hand ran over my wolf arm, I jerked.

"Don't," I whispered, afraid that if he touched me, he'd understand what an abomination I was.

His hand remained. "I've been holding you long enough to understand your curse," he said softly. "And it is not as horrible as you think. There is a symmetry to it that is fascinating."

I wanted to shrink in on myself.

"You are still beautiful in your own way." He reached up and stroked from my shoulders down to my fingers on my right arm and to my paw on my left. The feel of his fingertips on the underside of my paw was strange and comforting at the same time. "I've never felt anything like you."

"And how many women have you felt?" I snapped. The thought burned my skin, but I did not move.

"None. Not in the way your tone insinuates. You almost sound...jealous."

"I'm not."

"Mhm. If you say so."

I started to get up, and his arms wrapped around me again.

"Stay still."

This time he whispered it in my ear, and his breath tickled me as it flowed over my skin.

"My mother used to let me study her face in both human form and wolf form so I would know her by touch. And I did the same with my brother and sister, although they were a little less willing to sit still." His face transformed from the tilted smile to something more tragic. His lips pulled down in deep sadness. "I miss them."

Quiet settled between us.

"Where do you think they are?"

He laid his head back again. "I have no idea. My mother sent us in different directions and created a diversion for us. I don't think she made it out alive."

I squeezed his hand gently, and he put a little pressure back, but not a true squeeze, as if trying not to jostle my thumb.

He pulled free, and then he held his hands up in front of me. "I see by touch." He wiggled his fingers, trying to get the levity back into his voice, but it failed, so he just dropped his hands into my lap, lacing his own fingers together, encircling me with his arms in case I had any ideas of escaping and tending to the fire. "Being blind puts me at a disadvantage in a very visual world, but I've accepted it and chosen to live life under my terms. Just like you have."

"No. You are far more accepting than I am."

He just smiled and tilted his head up a little. "If you say so." And then his head dropped back again, and his eyes closed. "By the way, did you know you smell like strawberries and cream?"

"Really?"

"Mhm. It reminds me of one of my favorite desserts that my mother used to make."

"Huh." I leaned my head back on his shoulder, wondering whether Adam really was my shot at happiness. I didn't really care whether the curse was lifted, because he was truly special. I placed my hand over his as we drifted off.

BELLE Chapter 12

NOISE LIKE A HERD of buffalo running across a field snapped me from sleep. "Do you hear that?"

He stiffened behind me. "Think you might grab my pants?" he asked, his voice ladened with sleep. He stretched his arms above his head. "How long did we sleep?"

Darkness still shrouded the living room. "I don't know. It's either still dark out or we slept clear through an entire day."

"You slept through the entire day," Faith said from where they were huddled near us.

I reached for Adam's pants with muscles stiff from staying in the same position. If I was stiff, he had to be hurting as well. I put the fabric in his hands and stood up slowly before I stepped out of his way on legs that felt like unstable stilts.

Flame flickered in the distance, and my mouth went dry. Neither one of us were in any condition to outrun a forest fire. I hurried to the window while

Adam pulled on the pants, and I blinked at the torch-carrying crowd outside the gate.

Adam stood up next to the couch with his pants on. He took a wincing step toward where I stood. If he kept going, he'd run into my chair. I went to him and took his hand and led him through the maze of furniture, glad he could walk. But a deep fear rose inside me, stronger than what the scene outside manifested.

Now that he was mobile, Adam was going to leave.

I wouldn't stop him, if that was what he truly wished.

All thoughts of Adam disappeared the minute I swung the door open. The town had come to deliver their own version of twisted justice.

My annoyance flared beyond aggravation at the pack congregated just outside the magical barrier. Their interruption of what could have turned out to be a truly tender moment, one that could have saved me, was more than unwelcome. It was downright lethal. Enough to set my teeth on edge.

Their intent was clear from the flaming weapons they carried, and I scanned the faces I had known all my life. It looked as though the entire town had showed up to end us. When my gaze fell on the people I had considered friends, my heart squeezed. But the real impact didn't hit me until my gaze passed and then snapped back to my parents in the back row. They wielded torches, too.

"Dear God," I whispered as my anger morphed into despair.

"What is it?" Adam asked from beside me. He balanced on one leg, his other still tender, but well enough to support his weight after almost twenty hours of solid sleep.

"It looks like the entire town has come to slaughter me. Including my parents."

His face hardened and a low growl came from deep within his chest. "I'm well enough to fight."

I put my hand out against his bare chest, stopping him from stepping out of the safety of the house. "This isn't your fight."

"The hell it isn't. You risked your life to save me from those bastards." His hand covered mine, and he squeezed.

"You've entertained me, fed me, nursed me back to health, and made me feel like I have no limitations. I won't let you go out there alone."

"Adam." I sighed.

He threaded his hand through mine and held tight. "You can't shift. I can."

"No. They'll tear you apart."

"And they won't do that to you?"

I eyed the crowd. Their intent was clear in their stances, their rumblings, and their catcalls. *Kill the monster.*

Instead of answering his question, I said, "With everyone up front, the back is clear. You should go. Save yourself." I tried to dislodge his hand, but his grip was solid and unyielding.

"I can't do that." His voice was soft enough to pull my gaze to his sightless one.

"You have to." My chest squeezed at the thought of him getting hurt again, or worse, him dying. But he stubbornly shook his head. "Why won't you even consider it?"

He unclasped his hand and reached for my face, feeling the jagged lines of my partially formed wolf. When his fingers found my human lips, he leaned in and pressed his to them. It was gentle and sweet.

The crowd hushed at the sight and then roared their anger. A few shot flaming arrows at the house, but the magical barrier separating us from them stopped their arrows, dropping them to the ground, where their flames hissed out in the wet grass.

"Despite what they think, and even despite what you think about yourself, you have a good heart and that's what captured mine. I cannot let them slaughter you just because your outside is imperfect. Not when you are gentle and kind and perfect to me."

My heart stopped, and I stared at him, stunned. Before I could get my bearings and insist he leave, magic swirled around us. It was like being in the center of a tornado. And the witch who cursed me appeared on the walkway between us and the angry crowd. She stared at me with satisfied eyes.

Now I was doubly gobsmacked, and my mouth fell open. I quickly recovered and dropped my gaze to the ground with the humility that filled me.

"Sorceress, I am so sorry for my initial judgment of you and my unkind words." My apology came from the heart. The more I thought about how I had reacted to her, the more mortified at my behavior I had become.

The witch inclined her head, turned toward the angry crowd, and raised her arms. "Belle has more heart than I gave her credit for." Her gaze scanned the crowd. "I cursed her just as I cursed her grandfather so many years ago. And you, as a town, did not learn from either experience. You banished both of them, and if you had your way, you would have ripped her from existence, as you had done to her grandfather."

She turned to me and pointed. A bolt of power shot from her fingers, engulfing me.

I screamed as my bones transformed, reversing the shift,

settling my body back into human form. The agony of it drew sweat to my skin, even with the cool air brushing me. Behind me, I heard the squeaks and moans of the mice transforming as well.

"Stop! You're hurting her!" Adam cried, his voice full of panic. He couldn't see the transformations or know this pain was temporary, like a wolf's first shift. It righted the wrongs of the past and breathed new life into me. Silently, I vowed not to let the curse of vanity into my soul ever again.

"No, boy. I am lifting my curse. She truly earned your love before the last petal fell from the cursed rosebush. Unlike her grandfather, who remained bitter and angry and sought to destroy anyone who crossed his path, she accepted what she had become. She learned to live with her disabilities, and even, dare I say, thrive with them. And in doing so, found the compassion that had been locked away in the presence of these hideous and thought-poisoning townspeople. Belle, you have restored my faith in your royal bloodline."

By the time she finished her little speech, my vision had blurred and snapped back to normal. I lifted my hands, both human, and then felt the contours of my face with a soft laugh. My gaze snapped to hers. "Royal?"

"Yes. You have the blood of the originals running through your veins. And for the first time in centuries, a royal has transformed to become worthy enough to break the curse. I thought your grandfather would be able to, but he was too lost in his grief to break through."

I blinked and my eyes widened. The leather-bound book in the library. The story I could no longer stomach. It had detailed the story of how the original werewolf bloodline had been lost to time, but that someday it would be restored when a descendant successfully broke the curse. It was the history of my bloodline.

My legs wobbled, but they held fast when her gaze shifted to Adam. I swallowed hard at the intensity of her stare. I did not want anything bad to befall him. Another bolt shot out, encapsuling him before I could protect him.

The witch said, "You see more as a blind man than most with vision. And as a reward for being truly pure of heart, I can offer you a small reprieve from the darkness. Unfortunately, it can only be while you are in your wild form."

Adam bowed back from the power swirling through him, and as soon as it faded, he shifted and glanced up at me. His eyes widened as he took my uncursed form in from head to toe. He had felt my deformities even moments ago and the way his eyes caressed me warmed my soul.

He looked out at the witch and gave her a thankful nod. Then his eyes turned toward the crowd, still holding their weapons and still glaring at us like we deserved death. A low growl sounded, announcing his displeasure.

I put my hand on his head. "They fear what they don't understand."

Both Adam and the witch looked at me with cocked eyebrows, as if I had said something so profound it gave them pause. But it was the basis for the town's nasty ways. Even my mother had fallen to the weight of fear.

Then the witch turned toward the angry crowd and pushed her hands toward them. The magic protecting this place rolled out and over them, dousing the flames, turning their weapons to dust, and bringing them to their knees. "Until you can see with your hearts and not your eyes, you will be bound in darkness. Until compassion is truly your first instinct, you cannot shift."

People wailed and felt around them for others, clinging to their neighbors in the face of the sudden absence of sight.

The only one who still stood with her eyes locked on me was my mother. Tears flowed down her cheeks.

"Go back to your homes," the witch ordered. "This land is off-limits to anyone with ill intent. And if you as a group decide to come back to wreak your revenge on Belle and her beau, the minute you step on Denton property, you will be cursed the same way Belle was. But for you, there will be no second chance."

People trembled in their forced darkness.

The witch pointed at my mother. "You were spared not because you have compassion in your heart, but to lead them out of these lands," the witch said to my mother. "You stood by while they slaughtered your father, and would have done the same today had Belle not been fortunate enough to find love in her cursed state. For that, you get to witness the consequences. And unless your heart is pure, do not set foot on this property. Otherwise, you will befall the same fate as the rest of these vile creatures."

My mother's face paled, and she slowly nodded, taking my father's hand. In silence, the crowd joined hands and started back toward the town, with my mother leading the way.

Adam shifted back to human form and reached out, brushing my hand with his. "I am sorry about your family," he said softly.

"You are sweet," I said, still watching the procession. "I'm sure I'll see them again someday." At least I hoped I would. I didn't go as far to tell them they would love him once they got to know him, because I didn't know whether they could shed their core belief in pursuing perfection.

The witch turned back toward me. "The land is warded in a similar way that this house was. No one with ill intent will pass through."

"Thank you." I nodded. "Not only for the charms, but for helping me see beyond myself."

She smiled brightly, and then she became smoke that dissipated in the wind. I turned around, looking in the foyer at three very emotional servants. Herman wore a butler's coat, and his shoes were so shiny, I could see the reflections of all three of them in the black patent leather. He was thin and tall, but there was nothing noteworthy about him, except for Faith, clinging to his arm as though she couldn't get enough of him. Her red hair flowed wildly underneath her maid's hat. She put her head on his shoulder and blew me a kiss.

Chauncey stood next to the odd pair in his cook whites. He was still marveling over his hands, as if he could not believe his curse had been lifted. Finally, his gaze rose to mine, and he did a sweeping bow.

"My lady," he said with a reverence I did not deserve.

I giggled in response, holding Adam's hand a little tighter than before. "Please continue to call me Belle. 'My lady' is so formal."

He bowed again. "Yes, my la...Belle." He caught himself halfway through and smirked. "I will go see what you have in the kitchen and make a list. I believe we need to go into the nearest town besides Averyton to stock up on food and toiletries, and clothing for you, my...Belle," he said with a broad smile.

Faith unhooked herself from Herman and crossed to me, throwing her arms around me in an unexpected hug. "Thank you," she whispered in my ear.

I hugged her back. "It wasn't my doing." I glanced at Adam.

"Oh, honey, it was you allowing yourself to be you, despite your affliction." She squeezed again and stepped back. "We must be going to help Chauncey put together that list. I imagine we will be gone a couple of days." She smiled at me and looked pointedly at Adam with an eyebrow raised in that suggestive way that made my entire face heat.

I rolled my eyes at her. "We will make do."

"I'm sure you will, my dear." She and Herman gave me a nod and headed toward the kitchen in the back of the mansion.

Adam stepped closer. "Are we alone?"

I swung the door closed and took his hands. "Yes. How's your leg feeling?"

"My leg is fine." He broke my grip and ran his hands up both arms, feeling my human form. "Would it be terrible of me to ask if I can see your wolf?" he asked just before he pulled me close and planted a kiss on my lips. This time, it was not chaste or sweet like it had been when he thought we were going into battle. This time it was hot and insistent, and I gasped in response as his arms pressed me against his chest. His tongue dipped into my mouth, twirling with mine in the most delicious way, making me forget his question.

When he pulled away, I actually whined.

"And then you can show me around this house. Especially the library and the other places you are fond of."

"Adam." I sighed at the questioning tilt of his eyebrows.

"You can also show me where you expect me to sleep." His lips curved in such a way that I couldn't deny him. He had been in this house for a little more than a week and only just got to experience the living room, and this was such a small part of the house.

"Fine," I conceded and stepped back. Nerves bit at my skin. I hadn't shifted in years and an underlying fear coated my skin with heat.

Before I could shift myself, he shifted and his sharp blue eyes stared up at me, scanning me from head to toe before he stepped closer and nudged me.

"I don't know if I can fully shift." I bit my lips, studying his blue eyes and his white, gray, and black markings of a gray wolf. He was stunning, and I ran my palm over his head, scratching lightly behind his ear. He licked my hand and then backed up, still favoring his right leg despite his declaration that he was good.

I closed my eyes and searched deep for the magic that allowed me to shift. It hid in the center of my chest, but I could see shimmers of it in my mind's eye. I grabbed hold of it and threw open the doors shutting it off from me. They flew wide, and magic flowed into every cell. The shift was faster than it had ever been. When I opened my eyes, Adam's mouth hung open a fraction and his eyes danced with deep joy as they beheld me with my calico coat of white, gold, and gray tones.

He stepped close and nudged me tenderly before he circled me, then he stopped, stepping away as he looked at our surroundings.

I shifted back to human form because I wanted to walk and turn and touch with both hands. His massive wolf head turned back to me, and his wolf smile disappeared.

"You can stay in that form while I show you around." I laughed. "I want to walk and talk and twirl and dance. And later, I want to run in the woods and hunt with you. But right now, I am a little giddy having two legs and two arms."

The smile returned, and I led him into the kitchen, interrupting the trio as I showed Adam the layout of the first floor. When we got to the last room, I stood before it and hesitated.

"This is where I kept the cursed rosebush." I pushed the door open and stepped in, crossing slowly to the cases on the table. One was my grandfather's, withered and bare, and in the other, my rosebush still had one perfect rose with all its petals. The rest were shriveled up on the bottom of the box, but the single pink rose nearly sparkled in the case.

I glanced at Adam. "This shouldn't be."

Adam looked at the flower suspended in life and then at me and shifted back to human form. Reaching for my hand, he pulled me to him. "It's the perfect representation of you, full of life and heart and resilience."

This time, when he went to kiss me, I pulled back.

His sweet smile faded.

"Don't you want to see the library?"

He shook his head and brushed his lips on my cheek, moving to discover the curve of my ear with his tongue. His hands slid over my back and down to my ass, stopping. He stepped away, his breath heavy. He licked his lips and brought his hands up to my face, running the pads of his fingers over my cheeks, my jawbone and then finally, my lips.

"I um. I'd like to see..." He swallowed and then laughed. "I'm not very good at this, am I?"

I cupped his cheek and studied his face and the sudden tic in his cheek under his eye. I stepped closer and captured a soft kiss. "Are you trying to seduce me?" I asked, humor lacing my voice.

His face turned crimson, and he went to step away, but I hooked my arms around his waist, pulling him back against me.

"I'm not saying no. I just have never been...seduced."

His tight muscles relaxed at my words, and a dazzling smile graced his face. "Yes, I'm trying in my very awkward way to...to mate with you."

"So...you'd like to see our bedroom?"

He blinked, and his mouth opened and then closed. He cocked his head. "Our?"

"Is that too presumptuous of me?" Now I was the one who was worried about my choice of words.

His answer was a kiss, and this one burned like a wildfire. His hands tore at my clothing, not waiting for the tour to continue. And I responded, ripping at his shirt as well. His hands left me to strip his shirt off and then returned to my body as they studied every patch of exposed skin there was.

He kissed his way down my neck to the curve of my breasts. His hands gently cupped me, his thumbs traveled over my nipples, and he let out a low groan as they hardened with his touch.

"I thought you were beautiful before," he whispered and then took my nipple in his mouth, sucking gently.

His touch set me on fire, and I whispered his name like a prayer. He lowered to his knees in front of me, trailing kisses from my chest to the pants I had on. He tilted his head up, as if questioning me with his fingers paused on the clasp.

The gentleman in him did not wish to presume, but the outline in his pants told me he wanted me just as badly as I wanted him.

I reached for his fingers and helped him undo my pants. "I'm yours, if you'll have me," I whispered, afraid he might choose a different option, even with his desire on display.

He paused and put his head to my stomach, lowering my pants, inch by inch, as if he were questioning his desires. I stepped out of the trousers, and he tossed them away. When his hands returned to my legs, they had a shake in them.

I threaded my hands through his hair and then slowly dropped to my knees in front of him. The cold marble offset the heat radiating from me. I kissed him and pulled him on top of me as I stretched out on the floor.

Another searing kiss followed, and then his mouth and hands traveled down my body. He paused and gently caressed my core. "I can't see your reactions, so you need to tell me if I'm doing something you don't like."

"I will."

He lowered his mouth between my legs, testing me with his tongue until he found the spot that made me gasp. He grinned and continued to coax me with his mouth and his fingers until my satisfaction dripped and my core wanted more of him. All of him.

Adam kicked his pants off and crawled over me, lining himself up with his hand before he pressed into me slowly. He closed his eyes and tilted his head back, looking every bit as sexy as I had imagined during those dark days.

"Belle," he breathed softly as he thrust deep inside, tearing through what was left of my innocence.

A brief blaze of pain registered and then only pleasure as he draped himself over me and found my lips, kissing me as slowly as his hips moved. His languid motion soon sped up, matching the pace of his tongue. He pulled from my mouth, arching into me as he straightened his arms, giving in to the passion. I moved with him, crying out his name as my hands dug into his shoulders. We both peaked at the same moment with a cry that seemed to shake the foundation underneath us.

The roots of the rosebush crashed through the table and into the ground, shattering marble as it took root in the soil beneath, growing and blooming as though it, too, was free of the curse. It devoured my grandfather's box, the table, and nearly overtook the center of the room, flourishing like the fable had said. When the curse lifted, a beautiful rose garden would take root, wiping out the centuries of royal failures.

I stared at it as my chest heaved and tendrils of pleasure still echoed in my form.

Adam lay his head on my shoulder. "Damn, the earth moved," he whispered.

I burst out laughing. "The rosebush took root," I said, since he couldn't see. "But yes, you rocked my world, too."

He grinned sheepishly up at me. "I'm glad you saved me."

I caressed his lips with my fingers, and he kissed them. "We saved each other. Now, let's go finish the house tour, and then I want to see you hunt."

His grin was infectious as he helped me to my feet. I handed him his clothing and put on what was left of mine. I had to rip the shirt out of the growing rosebush and put on the torn fabric, considering the staff were still in the house.

As we stepped out of the rose room, Faith came running toward us.

"Are you two okay?" she asked, focusing on my ripped shirt.

I opened the door wide, and her gaze fell on the rosebush growing in the center of the room.

Her head snapped to me, and her eyebrows arched. "Well then," she replied and smiled, as if all was right with the world now. She bowed and scurried away, leaving us to mull her reaction together.

"I'm not sure I want to hunt tonight." Adam took my hand and sucked on a couple of my fingers. "How about you?"

My mind went fuzzy as I stared at his incorrigible grin. His unseeing eyes sparkled with mischief that I'd always dreamed of.

"I guess hunting can wait," I replied and led him by the hand to the grand bedroom, where I hadn't slept since the day I found him. The bed looked inviting, and I kicked the door closed behind us.

His lips toyed with a smile. "Did you bring me to the library?"

"Nope." I pulled him to the bed and pushed him back onto the soft mattress. "And it is my turn to discover all that you are."

He snorted a laugh and climbed backward into the center of the bed. "You've had a full view of my wares since day one."

I crawled onto the bed on top of him. "True, but I only looked. I didn't touch. Especially not the way I intend to touch you tonight."

Adam clasped his hands behind his head. "By all means, explore to your heart's content."

And I explored Adam until he was panting with need and then made sweet love to him, giving him a glimpse of the promise that lay ahead of us for the rest of our lives.

THE END

If you enjoyed BELLE: A FRACTURED FAIRY TALE, please consider leaving a review!

Find more books by J.E. Taylor on her website: http://books.jetaylor75.com/

About J.E. Taylor

J.E. Taylor is a USA Today bestselling author, a publisher, an editor, a manuscript formatter, a mother, a wife, a business analyst, and a Supernatural fangirl. Not necessarily in that order. She first sat down to seriously write in February of 2007 after her daughter asked:

"Mom, if you could do anything, what would you do?"

From that moment on, she hasn't looked back.

Besides being co-owner of Novel Concept Publishing, Ms. Taylor also moonlights as a Senior Editor of Allegory, an online venue for Science Fiction, Fantasy and Horror. J.E. Taylor is also one of the co-hosts of the popular podcast <u>Spilling Ink</u>.

She lives in New Hampshire with her husband and two children and during the summer months enjoys her weekends on the shore in southern Maine.

Visit her at <u>www.books.jetaylor75.com</u> and sign up for her newsletter for early previews of her upcoming books!

If you liked BELLE, you might also like these other fairy tales and magical romance stories from J.E. Taylor's backlist:

A FRACTURED FAIRY TALE

BOOKS 1-10

Little Red Riding Hood, Cinderella, Brave, Rapunzel, Frozen, Snow White, Sleeping Beauty, Aladdin, Beauty and the Beast and Peter Pan – all fairy tales you know and love, but twisted, fractured into something new.

Shifters and magic claw through the pages of these fractured fairy tales, giving you a thrilling take on an old tale.

Will the heroine survive whatever the evil villain has in store? Or will Love conquer all?

Grab your hardcover edition of A Fractured Fairy Tale—books 1-10 and find out!

A Fractured Fairy Tale books 1-10 includes

Red, Cinder, Brave, Tangled, Frozen, Snow, Spindle, Jasmine, Belle, Hook

Find these titles and other fantasy and suspense titles on J.E. Taylor's website!

https://JETaylor75.com